The
Twelve Dancing
Princesses

Retold by Emma Helbrough

Illustrated by
Anna Luraschi

Reading Consultant: Alison Kelly
University of Surrey Roehampton

Contents

Chapter 1

Family trouble

There were once twelve beautiful princesses, all with long, flowing hair and short, fiery tempers.

Their father, the king, was a grumpy old man who didn't believe in having fun.

In fact, he believed that princesses should be seen and not heard.

Ballroom →

NO ENTRY

The princesses strongly disagreed.

5

The thing they argued
about most was dancing.
Their father hated it, but
the princesses loved it...

so whenever
he wasn't
looking,
they danced
anyway.

Chapter 2

The sisters' secret

The girls slept in a tall tower
with their beds side by side.

Every night, the king locked
the tower door, so that they
couldn't sneak out.

Sleep well,
my dears.

One morning, when the door was unlocked, the princesses were still asleep.

As the maid went to wake them, she noticed their shoes were lying in a soggy pile on the floor.

How strange!

The shoes were worn out.

When the king heard about the shoes, he was furious. "Those girls have been out dancing," he spluttered.

Bring my daughters here... NOW!

Yes, sire.

"Princesses should not be out dancing all night!" he yelled at them. "You need your beauty sleep. You should all be ashamed of yourselves."

The girls weren't ashamed in the least. What's more, they wouldn't tell him how they had escaped or where they had been.

11

The next morning, it was clear that the princesses had been out again. The same thing happened seven nights in a row.

The king didn't know what to do.

Then he had a brilliant idea.

He decided that the first man to discover where his daughters went each night could marry one of them. Posters went up across the land.

Fed up with your job? Feel like a challenge?

Solve a royal mystery and win big prizes!!

Win your own kingdom and marry a genuine princess!

Interested? Drop in to the castle for further details.

No time wasters please.

Chapter 3

Taking the challenge

The first man to take up the
king's challenge was brave
Prince Marcus.

"By the way, there is one small catch," the king told him. "If you fail, I'll cut off your head!"

Um…okay…
no problem, your
majesty.

15

That night, Prince Marcus was taken to the tower and put in a room next to the princesses.

Very comfortable indeed!

They made him very welcome. One even brought him a cup of hot, milky cocoa.

As Prince Marcus drank the cocoa, he began to feel sleepy.

He tried splashing cold water on his face, but that didn't work.

Soon he was fast asleep and snoring loudly.

Next morning, the princesses' shoes were worn out again. Prince Marcus had failed – and the king wasn't joking about chopping off his head.

Take him away!

Many more princes and noble knights came forward. But they were all fooled by the princesses' sweet smiles...

and their offer of hot cocoa.

Chapter 4

Ralph and Rascal

One day, a magician named Ralph and his pet dog, Rascal, were passing the castle.

Ralph noticed one of the king's posters and decided to find out more.

This could be interesting, Rascal!

21

When he saw Ralph, the king looked doubtful. But he was desperate to know what the girls were up to, so he agreed to let Ralph try.

I'll chop off your head if you fail, you know.

Yes, but I won't fail...

Night came and Ralph was put in the same room where the others had stayed.

"Hello! I'm Amy," said the youngest. "He's nice," she whispered to her sisters. "I don't want him to die because of us. Maybe we shouldn't go out tonight..."

Her sisters ignored her.

A few minutes later, Annabel, the eldest sister, brought Ralph a cup of cocoa. But Ralph was a wise magician. He knew what she was up to.

He pretended to drink the cocoa. Then, when Annabel wasn't looking, he poured it into Rascal's bowl. Rascal was delighted.

Ralph yawned. "I think I'll just put my feet up for a few minutes," he told Annabel.

Then, with an even bigger yawn, he pretended to fall fast asleep.

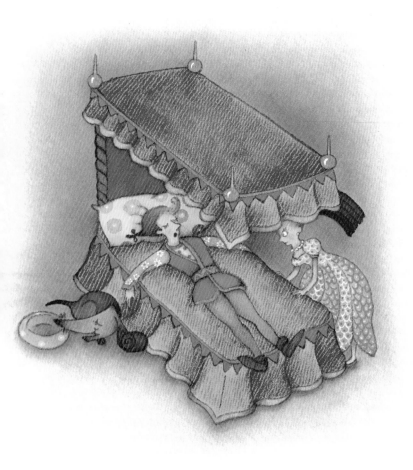

Annabel crept back to her sisters. "He's asleep," she whispered. "Let's get ready!"

They put on their sparkliest ball dresses...

and new shoes. The princesses shimmered like a rainbow.

27

With the last button
buttoned and the last bow
tied, the girls stood by their
beds. Annabel pulled back a
dusty, old rug in the corner
of the room to reveal a
secret trap door. The
hinges creaked as
she pulled it open.

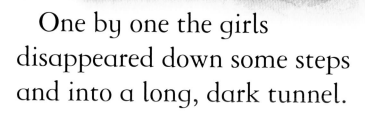

One by one the girls
disappeared down some steps
and into a long, dark tunnel.

Chapter 5

Ralph on the trail

When the princesses were out of sight, Ralph quickly entered their room.

He clicked his fingers and a cloak appeared. With a second click, Ralph vanished.

Carefully, he tiptoed down the steps into the tunnel.

It didn't take long for him to catch up with the princesses.

Ralph tried to walk quietly,
but it wasn't easy. At one
point he stepped on Amy's
dress. She jumped and turned
around, but there was no
one there...

A few moments later Ralph stepped on a twig. Now Amy was convinced that someone was following them. Her sisters didn't believe her.

At the end of the tunnel they came to an astonishing row of trees.

Some of the trees glistened with silver...

some with gold...

and some with sparkling diamonds.

33

Ralph had never seen trees
like them. While the princesses
carried on, he gently broke
off a twig from each tree.

Up ahead, the princesses had
stopped before a lake. It stood in
the shadow of a beautiful castle.

Twelve boats were
waiting at the edge
of the lake and in
each boat sat a
handsome prince.

Each prince rowed a princess
across the lake.

35

Ralph sneaked into the boat carrying Amy. When they reached the other side, a band began to play.

The princesses danced until
their feet were sore and
the soles of their shoes
were worn through.

As the sun rose, they limped home. "Our nights of dancing are still safe – unlike poor Ralph's head!" said Annabel, yawning. Amy looked upset.

Chapter 6

A shock for the king

The king was having breakfast
when Ralph strolled in. "Good
morning, your majesty," said
Ralph brightly.

"I suppose you've come to tell me you failed too," sighed the king.

"Ah, but I didn't, sire," Ralph replied. Waving the twigs, he told the king what he'd seen.

"This all sounds very unlikely," grumbled the king, when Ralph had finished. "Are you sure you're not just making it up to save your head?"

He decided to call for
Annabel. When she saw the
three twigs in his hand, she
looked horrified.

One look at her face told the
king all he needed to know.
"Dancing is banned!" he declared.

The princesses sobbed and wailed when they heard their secret had been discovered.

"What will we do?" they cried. "Life is so dull without dancing."

This is the worst day of my life.

But there was nothing they could do.

True to his word, the king let Ralph marry one of his daughters. "I'd like Amy," Ralph said, "if she'll have me. She's the sweetest of all."

I'm sure you'll both be very happy.

Amy and Ralph's wedding was a joyful occasion. Even the king couldn't stop smiling. "I have a surprise for you," he whispered to Amy.

The king led her to the
ballroom and Amy gasped.
Hundreds of candles lit up
the dance floor and in
the corner a band was
playing a lively tune.

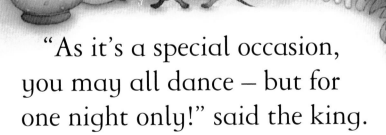

"As it's a special occasion,
you may all dance – but for
one night only!" said the king.

"Oh, how wonderful!" cried Amy and her sisters, grabbing partners. They were all still dancing the following night.

"I thought I said one night only!" said the king, but he smiled. Ralph had worked some more of his magic.

The Twelve Dancing Princesses was first
written down by two brothers, Jacob and
Wilhelm Grimm. They lived in Germany
in the early 1800s and together they
retold hundreds of fairy tales.

Series editor: Lesley Sims

Designed by Russell Punter
and Natacha Goransky

First published in 2004 by Usborne Publishing Ltd., Usborne House,
83-85 Saffron Hill, London EC1N 8RT, England. www.usborne.com
Copyright © 2004 Usborne Publishing Ltd.